CA... N

Pinnacle
COCKFOST...
La Perous...
OAKWOOD

EDGWARE
BURNT OAK
COLINDALE
HENDON CENT...
...BLEY PARK
BREN...
...NEASDEN
DOLLIS HILL
WILLESDEN
KILBURN...
WE...

MILL HILL
Johnston Atoll
U.S.

BOUNDS GREEN
WOOD GREEN
TURNPIKE LANE
MANOR HOUSE
...BURY PARK
...ARSENAL
FINS...
A...
DRA...
HIGHBU...
ISLINGT...
HOLLOWAY ROAD
...LEDONIAN ROAD

...CENTRAL
...T CROSS
GOLDERS GREEN
HAMPSTEAD
BELSIZE PA...
CHAL...
GREEN

Atoll
...oll
...irik Atoll
...iluk Atoll
Wotje Atoll
Maloelap Ato...
Aur Atoll
Arno Atoll
Majuro Atoll
Mili Atoll
...Island Atoll
Makin
...o Marakei
...baiang
...Maiana
Nonouti
Tabiteuea
...ngsmill Group
...Tama...
GI...
Tara...
Abe...

MAR...
...SHALL
...oll
...ISLANDS
...6
MARYLEBONE
EDGWARE ROAD
MARBLE ARCH
LANCASTER GATE
HYDE PARK CORNER
...BRIDGE
SLOANE SQUARE
...OUTH ...INGTON
PIMLICO

...BERT
...wa Atoll
...emama 10
...BI...
...ST...
...BOND STREET
...GREEN PARK
ISLANDS
Beru 8
...ana
Arorae 15
Nanumea
Niutao
Nanumanga
Nui
Vaitupu
Nukufetau
Funafuti Atoll
Nukulaelae
Nurakita
ELLICE ISLANDS
U.K.
...HA-M-E...

ST HAMPSTEAD
FINCHLEY ROAD
SWISS COTTAGE
ST. JOHN'S WO...
BAKER STREET
GREAT PORTLAND STREET
REGENT'S PARK
...OND STREET
PICCADILLY CIRC...
ST. JAMES'S PARK
VICTORIA
WES...
...AU ISLANDS
(...ON GROUP)
VAUXHA...
...anger Is.

EQUATO...
...ration
...bury I. 33
CHA...
...oint Administ...
Phoenix I.
...15
...ISLANDS
New Zealand
Admi...
...N
...fu
...nono
...Fakaofo

British Rail
ESSEX ROA...
OLD STREET
MOORGATE
BANK
LIVERPOOL STREET
ALDGATE
TOWER HILL
LONDON BRIDGE
ESCALATOR LINK

...and
...land
...island.
Enderb...
...rnie I.
...and
...ministered by N...
TOKELA...
(UNIO...
Swains I.
D...
BOROUGH

Ender...
Phoe...
Sydney I.
Mansion House
PHOENIX IS...

HOLLOWAY ROAD
...LEDONIAN ROAD
ANGEL
...RRINGDON
...ELL ...ARE
BARBICAN
...HANCERY LANE
ST. PAUL'S
Waterloo & City Line
MONUMEN...
MANSION HOUSE
CANNON STREET
...RIARS
BOROUGH

GRIFFIN&SABINE

GRIFFIN&SABINE

An Extraordinary Correspondence

10TH ANNIVERSARY LIMITED EDITION

by Nick Bantock

CHRONICLE BOOKS

SAN FRANCISCO

Library of Congress Cataloging-in-Publication Data:

Bantock, Nick.
Griffin & Sabine : an extraordinary correspondence /
by Nick Bantock—10th anniversary limited ed.
p. cm.

ISBN 0-8118-3200-7

1. Artists—Fiction. 2. Imaginary letters. 3. Toy and movable
books—Specimens. I. Title: Griffin and Sabine. II. Title.
PR6052.A54 G75 2001
823'.914—dc21   2001017187

Printed in Hong Kong.

10 9 8 7 6 5 4 3 2 1

Chronicle Books LLC
85 Second Street
San Francisco, California 94105

www.chroniclebooks.com

For Kim Kasasian

With special thanks to all those readers who've become
intimately attached to Griffin and Sabine

Griffin Moss
It's good to get in touch
with you at last.
Could I have one of your
fish postcards?
I think you were right —
the wine glass has more impact
than the cup.
                    Sabine Strohem

P.O. Box 1. Katie. Sicmon Islands. South Pacific.

Griffin Moss. Gryphon Cards
41 Yeats Avenue
London
N.W.3
England.

22 FEB

SABINE
THANK YOU FOR YOUR EXOTIC
POSTCARD. FORGIVE ME IF
IT'S A MEMORY LAPSE ON MY
PART, BUT SHOULD I KNOW
YOU?
I CAN'T FATHOM OUT HOW YOU
WERE AWARE OF MY FIRST,
BROKEN CUP, SKETCH FOR THIS
CARD. I DON'T REMEMBER
SHOWING IT TO ANYONE.
PLEASE ENLIGHTEN ME.
                    YOURS
                    GRIFFIN MOSS

GRYPHON CARDS

SABINE STROHEM
P.O. BOX ONE F
KATIE
SICMON ISLANDS
SOUTH PACIFIC

By air mail
Par avion

Drinking Like a Fish

Griffin Moss

No, Griffin, you don't know me, not
in the way you mean, though I've
been watching your art for many years.
Having finally established who and
where you are, I feel compelled to
reveal myself.

The phenomenon that links us has taught me much
about you, yet I am ignorant of your history.
Please tell me something of your life.

It is such a pleasure having your images in a
tangible form. I really like the kangeroo in the hat,
but I wonder whether you should have darkened
the sky ?   Sabine

Griffin Moss
41 Yeats Avenue
London
N.W. 3
England

MS. STROHEM   15 MARCH

WHAT'S GOING ON? HOW IN THE WORLD
COULD YOU KNOW I DARKENED THE SKY
BEHIND THE KANGEROO? IT WAS ONLY A
LIGHT COBALT FOR ABOUT HALF AN HOUR.
AND WHAT DO YOU MEAN BY "PHENOMENON"
AND TANGIBLE"?

OK. IF GETTING ME INTRIGUED IS WHAT
YOU'RE AFTER, YOU'VE SUCCEEDED, BUT
YOU CAN HARDLY EXPECT ME TO SPILL MY
LIFE STORY TO A STRANGER.

WHY ARE YOU BEING SO RUDDY
MYSTERIOUS?

               GRIFFIN MOSS

           GRYPHON CARDS

P.S. YOUR POSTCARDS ARE
HANDMADE - DID YOU DO THEM
YOURSELF?

Air Mail Par avion

SABINE STROHEM
PO BOX ONE F
KATIE
SICMON ISLS.
SOUTH PACIFIC

13ᵖ

Griffin - you're right. I am being mysterious, but I assure
you it's for good reason. What I have to say will be
disturbing, and I wish you no distress.
I share your sight. When you draw and paint, I see what
you're doing while you do it. I know your work almost
as well as I know my own. Of course I do not expect
you to believe this without proof :
Last week while working on a head in
chalk, you paused and lightly sketched
a bird in the bottom corner of the
paper. You then erased it, and
obliterated all trace with heavy black.
Don't be alarmed — I wish you only well.

                                Sabine

Yes the pictures on the cards are mine.

Griffin Moss
41 Yeats Avenue
London
N.W. 3
England.

SABINE/   16 APRIL
THIS IS IMPOSSIBLE, AND YET IT MUST BE TRUE.
THERE WAS NO ONE IN MY STUDIO ALL THAT WEEK,
LET ALONE WHEN I SCRIBBLED THE BIRD. I'VE
CHECKED THE DRAWING AND THERE'S NOT THE
SLIGHTEST SIGN OF THE CREATURE FRONT OR
BACK. GOD KNOWS HOW, BUT YOU REALLY CAN
SEE ME, CAN'T YOU?
WHY DOESN'T THIS ALARM ME AS MUCH AS IT
SHOULD? I SUPPOSE BECAUSE I'VE ALWAYS
SENSED THAT I WAS BEING WATCHED, BUT I'D PUT IT
DOWN TO EVERYDAY PARANOIA.
I'VE A MILLION QUESTIONS. AM I
THE ONLY ONE YOU SEE? WHAT FORM
DOES YOUR SIGHT TAKE?
HOW COME I CAN'T SEE YOU?

GRYPHON CARDS

I WANT TO HEAR EVERYTHING.
WRITE IN DETAIL. TELL ME ALL
ABOUT YOURSELF. I DEMAND
TO KNOW —   PLEASE.

                    GRIFFIN

SABINE STROHEM
P.O. BOX 1F
KATIE
SICMON ISLANDS
SOUTH PACIFIC

BY AIR MAIL
PAR AVION

3ᴾ

10ᴾ